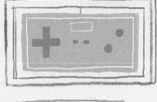

CINDERFELLA

TO ALL THE BROTHERS AT NUMBER 12 —
YOU'RE INVITED TO KAYLEIGH'S PARTY.
DRESS FANCY!

COME FANCY!

DANCE!

Malachy Doyle

illustrated by Matt Hunt

For Daniel, Nuala,
Jonah and Bryn
M.D.

For my family
M.H.

First published 2018 by Walker Books Ltd
87 Vauxhall Walk, London SE11 5HJ

2 4 6 8 10 9 7 5 3 1

Text © 2018 Malachy Doyle · Illustrations © 2018 Matt Hunt

The right of Malachy Doyle and Matt Hunt to be identified as
author and illustrator respectively of this work has been asserted by
them in accordance with the Copyright, Designs and Patents Act 1988

This book has been typeset in Blue Sheep

Printed in China

British Library Cataloguing in Publication Data:
a catalogue record for this book is available from the British Library

ISBN 978-1-4063-5654-0 (hb) · ISBN 978-1-4063-7063-8 (pb)

www.walker.co.uk

CINDERFELLA

Malachy Doyle
illustrated by Matt Hunt

WALKER BOOKS
AND SUBSIDIARIES
LONDON · BOSTON · SYDNEY · AUCKLAND

Once upon a day, there were three brothers. And once upon every night, at eight o'clock sharp, the two older ones, Gareth and Gus, went off to their ever-so-cosy beds.

The youngest, though, had to spend the night as close as he could to the fire with his little dog, Ruff.

And that's why they called him...

Cinderfella. Cinder-do-every-job-in-the-house-fella!

"Turn up the TV, shrimp," shouted Gareth.
"And put out the bins!"

"Then order us a mega-pizza,"
yelled Gus. "We're starving!"

BOOM!

ZOOM!

BANG!

"Oh, Ruff," said Cinderfella.
"They're just such bossy
brothers, aren't they?"

"Ruff, ruff!" said Ruff.

And no matter how hard Cinderfella worked,
the other two never stopped yelling at him...

Yes, Gareth and Gus were SO bossy.
Especially on the day that Kayleigh –
the junior karate champ – was having her party.

"Shine our scooters, then iron our outfits, Cinders!" ordered Gareth.

"Yeah, Kayleigh's having a dance tonight," sneered Gus, "and guess who's not invited?"

"I wish Kayleigh had asked us, Ruff," said Cinderfella, as the brothers scooted off. "We're much better dancers than those two..."

And that's when he noticed Ruff had a piece of paper in her mouth.

"Hey, what have you got there?" asked Cinderfella, as he began to read...

"That includes me!
Kayleigh invited
ME as well!"

"*Ruff, ruff!*" said Ruff.

Ruff rushed over to Gus and Gareth's wardrobe.

"These'll look cool at the party!" cried Cinderfella, trying on some sunglasses.

"Now Gareth and Gus won't even know who we are. We've just got to make sure we're back home before they are."

Ruff, meanwhile, had found some sparkly wheels.

"Good idea," said Cinderfella. "We'll go on that!"

At the party, everyone was doing the *Groovy Chicken*.
Well, almost everyone...

"It's your lucky night, Kayleigh –
come and dance with me!" said Gareth.

"It is indeed," cried Gus,
strutting up and down. "Because I, Gus,
am here to dance you to dreamland!"

"Oh, these lookalike boys and their copycat dancing," sighed Kayleigh.

Then she spotted someone on the other side of the room.

"Who's that?" she asked the brothers ... but neither of them knew.

"Hey," she said, gliding over. "I like your moves ... and your dog's!"

"Thanks," said Cinderfella, grinning. "We're doing the *Funky Monkey!*"

"Can I do it, too?" asked Kayleigh, taking him by the hand.

The two of them hopped and they bopped, they giggled and grooved...

Hop banana, jump banana ...

S-k-i-d banana ...

swing from the trees ...   and land on your knees!

s-l-i-d-e banana...

We're doing the Funky Monkey!

They were singing and swinging until
Cinderfella's watch beeped eight times.
Suddenly he remembered ...
he had to be back before
Gus and Gareth's bedtime!

"See you later,
Kayleigh Karate-Chop!"
he said, slicing her
a high-five.

But as he and Ruff
sped off ...
his sunglasses
went flying.

And, a little while later,
Kayleigh found them.

"I wish they could have stayed,"
she said, picking up the shades.

And so
it came about
that Kayleigh ...

spent all weekend scouring the neighbourhood, searching for Cinderfella.

... and every boy she met had to try on the fancy glasses, to see if it was him ...

(no matter how silly they looked.)

STORE

The very last house
Kayleigh came to
belonged to Gareth
and Gus ... and Cinderfella.

"Does that funky dancing
boy live here?" she gasped.
"The one who was wearing
these specs?"

"That was ME!" cried Gareth
and Gus, trying them on.

Kayleigh shook her head.
"No way! Oh, I'm never
going to find him."

Then, all of a sudden,
she heard a ...

"Hey!" cried Kayleigh. "That sounds like the little dog. That funky dancing dog!"

"Oh, no," said the brothers, blocking the doorway. "It can't be."

But Kayleigh knew that it was.
With a mighty 'Hai – YAH!' she burst open the door and there on the other side ... was Ruff.

And who was behind her?

RUFF! RUFF!

Sure enough,
it was Cinderfella,
lighting up the room.

With a happy 'Hai – YAH!'
Kayleigh popped the
glasses back onto
his nose.

"I finally found you!"
she cried.

"Let's bop till we drop, Karate-Chop!"
said Cinderfella, with the
grinniest of grins.

Now, happily ever after, they're the best of funky friends, singing ...

"Kick banana! Chop banana!
We're doing the Funky Monkey!"

THE END